NICK BUTTERWORTH

Q Pootle 5

GROOBIE'S SPACEWASH

WALKER
ENTERTAINMENT

Pootle 5 arrived at Groobie's to find him busy with a hammer. Bang! Bang! Bang!

"Hello Groobie," said Pootle. "Oopsy just told me about your spacewash. Her spaceship looks sooo clean!"

"Ah! This spacewash may look old, but it's got a few washes in it yet," said Groobie.

"It's a lean, mean, cleaning machine," said Bud-D, excitedly.

"Do you fancy giving it a try?" asked Groobie.

Pootle shook his head as he turned to go.

"No thanks, Groobie. I'll stick to my bucket and sponge."

roobie turned to his robot friend.

"OK, Bud-D. Let's get to work!"

Bud-D began calling, loudly, through a megaphone.

"Spacewash! Spacewash! Come and get it!"

Almost at once, Stella arrived with Ray.

id someone say 'spacewash'?"
she said.
"Your spaceship will be as clean as
a whistle!" beamed Groobie.
"Let's give it a try!" said Stella.

tella flew into
the spacewash.
She waited. Everything
was quiet.

"Hello?" Stella's voice
echoed. "Nothing's
happening."

Groobie pressed a
large button on the
spacewash control
panel.

"It is *now*!"

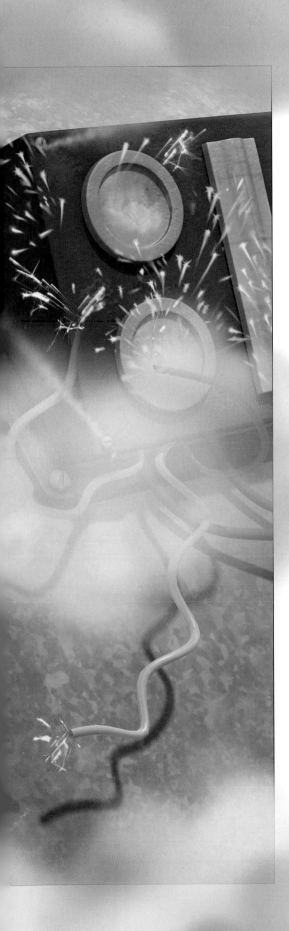

ssssss . . . phfsssssssssss! Wheeeeeeeeeeee! Swooooooooosh! Phfsssssssss! Grrr-grrr! Keruuunch!

Groobie looked concerned.

"They should be out by now."

He pulled a lever and jabbed at more buttons. The machine shuddered, and sparks flew everywhere. Steam hissed, and smoke billowed into the air.

Whssssssssss! Swoooooooosh! Grrrrungg! BANG!!! Spitz!! Spitzz! Bzzzrrrrrrr...

Silence.

"GROOBIE!" Stella spluttered.

"GET US OUT!"

Pootle was pootling about in space when he got the call for help.

"This is Groobie to Q Pootle 5. We have a slight problem. Could you help? I repeat . . . We need help!"

"I hear you, Groobie," Pootle radioed. "I'm on my way!"

t the spacewash, Eddi had arrived
and was trying to be helpful.

"Have you tried going backwards?" he called
to Stella.

"Yes." Stella sounded just a little bit cross.

"What about sideways?"

"Now you're being silly." Stella definitely
was cross. Eddi looked at Groobie.

"There's only one thing for it."
Eddi climbed into his
spaceship and pointed it
at the dark entrance to
the spacewash.

ddi revved, charged and disappeared. There was a loud CLUNK! and Stella's spaceship burst from the other end of the spacewash.

tella looked wet and bedraggled.

Suddenly, beside her, Ray popped up like a Jack-in-a-box, wearing a feathery, new hairdo. Bud-D primped it carefully.

"All part of the service!" he said.

"I'm going home for a bath," said Stella. "And Ray needs a haircut."

Pootle landed and ran over to Groobie.

"Panic over," said Groobie, "Stella and Ray are free from the spacewash."

Pootle tried hard not to giggle.

"So I can see," he said.

ow did you get them out?" Pootle asked.

"It was Eddi!" said Bud-D.

"Yes," said Groobie. "He flew right inside the spacewash and pushed Stella and Ray out. They went, POP!"

"Well done, Eddi!" said Pootle. "Er . . . where is Eddi . . ?"

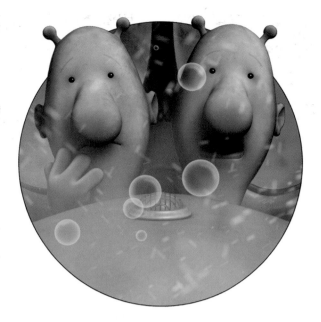

HEEEEELP!" Eddi wailed. "I'M STUCK!"

"Hang on in there, Eddi," Pootle called. "We're going to get you out."

Pootle jumped up to the spacewash controls and pressed a few buttons.

Nothing happened. He pulled a lever, but it broke off in his hand.

"How *are* we going to get him out?" asked Groobie.

Pootle thought hard.

"By all pulling together!" he said.

Pootle and his friends lined up their spaceships in front of the spacewash. Pootle roped the spaceships together and tied the rope to a plunger.

"Okay, Eddi!" Pootle took aim. "Here it comes!"

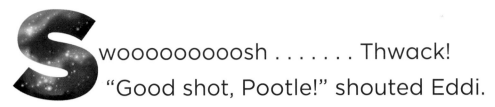

Swooooooooosh . . . . Thwack!

"Good shot, Pootle!" shouted Eddi.

Pootle ran to his spaceship and fired up the boosters.

"Ready everyone?" Everyone was ready.

"Brace yourself, Eddi," Pootle shouted.

"I'm bracing!" Eddi called back.

rom Stella, to Oopsy, to Groobie, to Pootle, the spaceships lifted from the ground and began to pull. The rope tightened.

"Increase thrust!" Pootle called.

The noise from the spaceships grew louder.

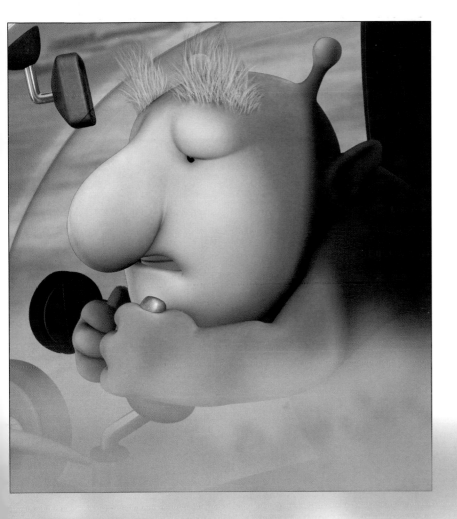

ore!" Pootle shouted over the din.
"One last pull!"
The spaceships roared and pulled. With a sudden grinding noise, something, somewhere, gave way. All at once, the spaceships lurched forward . . .

CRASH! BANG!! KERUMP!!!

Eddi's spaceship shot
out of the spacewash.
He was free!

As the spacewash had broken down, and Pootle was the only one with a bucket and sponge, he offered to wash all the dusty, dirty spaceships.

"You're very kind, Pootle," said Groobie.

"That's okay," Pootle smiled. "I'm sorry about your spacewash."

"Oh, I've moved on from that," said Groobie.

"Moved on? What …" Pootle suddenly noticed that the spacewash was working again.

t that very moment, with a clunk and
a hiss of steam, a very happy looking
Oopsy flew out. Pootle's mouth dropped open
in amazement.

"Oopsy! Your hair!"

"Do you like it?" she giggled.

Groobie beamed. "Welcome to Groobie's
Fly-Thru Hair Salon!"
he said.

Did you spot the space mice in this book?

You have to look carefully. They're very good at hiding!

Text by Nick Butterworth, based on the television series episode *Groobie's Spacewash*, written by Dave Ingham
Images composed by Nick Butterworth and Dan Cripps, produced by series animators Blue Zoo

First published 2014 by Walker Entertainment, an imprint of Walker Books Ltd
87 Vauxhall Walk, London SE11 5HJ

2 4 6 8 10 9 7 5 3 1

This book has been typeset in Gotham Book

Printed in Humen, Dongguan, China

British Library Cataloguing in Publication Data:
a catalogue record for this book is available from the British Library

ISBN 978-1-4063-5902-2

www.walker.co.uk

www.QPOOTLE5.com